ER PER

P9-CKW-861

PERLE, RUTH LERNER

ZIGGY AND THE ZIG-ZAG RACE
C1991

Emmy
the Exaggerating
Elephant

Fenton
the Fearful Frog

Gert
the Grungy Goat

the Happy
Hamster

the Impatient
Iguana

Ollie
the Obedient
Ostrich

Perry
the Polite
Porcupine

Queenie
the Quiet Quail

Rupert
the Resourceful
Rhinoceros

Ziggy
the Zippy Zebra

Wendy
the Wise
Woodchuck

Xavier
the X-ploring
Xenops

Yori
the Yucky Yak

NOTE TO PARENTS

Ziggy and the Zig-Zag Race
A story about the importance of health, fitness, and doing your best

In this story, Ziggy the Zippy Zebra hopes to win the annual Zig-Zag Race. He continues his daily exercises and practices good health habits, but he suddenly gets the jitters when he sees some of his friends getting ready for the race, too. With the help of Wendy the Wise Woodchuck, Ziggy regains his confidence and discovers that by doing his very best, he can win the race.

In addition to enjoying this humorous story with your child, you can use it to teach a gentle lesson about the importance of having good daily health habits—eating nutritious foods, exercising, and getting enough sleep.

You can also use this story to introduce the letter **Z**. As you read about Ziggy the Zippy Zebra, ask your child to listen for all the words that start with **Z** and point to the objects that begin with **Z**. When you've finished reading the story, your child will enjoy doing the activity at the end of the book.

DRIFTWOOD PUBLIC LIBRARY
801 SW HWY. 101
LINCOLN CITY, OREGON 97367

The AlphaPets™ characters were conceived and created by Ruth Lerner Perle.
Characters interpreted and designed by Deborah Colvin Borgo.
Cover/book design and production by Norton & Company.
Logo design by Deborah Colvin Borgo and Nancy S. Norton.
Edited by Ruth Lerner Perle.

Grolier Books is a Division of Grolier Enterprises, Inc.   Printed and Manufactured in the United States of America
Copyright © 1992 by Graymont Enterprises, Inc. No part of this work may be reproduced or adapted in any manner or medium whatever without the express written permission of Graymont Enterprises, Inc. AlphaPets and the AlphaPets characters are trade and service marks of Graymont Enterprises, Inc.

Ziggy and the Zig-Zag Race

ANN DEE HARDY

Illustrated by Judy Blankenship

GROLIER
BOOKS

Ziggy the Zippy Zebra was about to leave the Zig-Zag Health Club when he saw a poster and some notices announcing the annual Three-Mile Zig-Zag Race. As usual, the first prize was a gold trophy, but *this* year the winner would also get a ride in a zeppelin.

"Zowie! I'll tell all my friends," said Ziggy. "I know they'll want to come and watch me run in the race."

Ziggy picked up a handful of announcements and left the club.

The next morning Ziggy did his wake-up exercises, took a shower, and had his usual nutritious breakfast of cereal, milk, fruit, and toast. While he ate, he read the announcement carefully.

"I can deliver these with the mail," Ziggy thought. "That way everybody will know about the race and come to cheer me on." He picked up the announcements and ran off to work at the post office.

When Ziggy got to work, he sorted stacks of letters by zip code. Zero-zero-one ... zero-zero-two ... zero-zero-three ...

Then he put all the mail into his mailbag. He put the announcements in his pocket, jumped on his bike, and started on his delivery route.

Along the way, Ziggy saw some of his friends.

Delilah the Demanding Duck
was playing her zither.

Herbie the Happy Hamster was
helping Lizzy the Lazy Lamb
pick zucchini.

Emmy the Exaggerating Elephant
was busy planting hundreds of zinnias.

And Ivy the Impatient Iguana
was sewing a zipper in her shorts.

Ziggy gave everyone their mail and said, "The Zig-Zag
Race is next Saturday. Come and watch me run! First
prize is a trophy and a ride in a zeppelin.!!"

Ziggy's last stop was at Tina the Truthful Tiger's house. As he put her mail in her mailbox, Ziggy heard voices counting, "8 . . . 9 . . . 10 . . . 11." Ziggy looked in the side yard and saw Tina and Ollie the Obedient Ostrich doing jumping jacks. "Zowie! They must be getting ready for the race, too," thought Ziggy. "They both finished right behind me last year."

Suddenly Ziggy got the jitters. "Hmm ... what if Tina or Ollie win the race?" he thought. "They've been exercising at the club a lot lately. Maybe one of them can run faster than I can. Maybe one of them will win the zeppelin ride."

Ziggy didn't like that thought at all. He was very upset as he rode off on his bicycle.

When Ziggy went to the Zig-Zag Health Club later that afternoon, he was surprised to see so many of the AlphaPets there.

Herbie was rowing on a rowing machine and so was Monty the Mimicking Mouse. Emmy was jogging on the treadmill. Delilah and Ivy were pedaling on exercise bicycles. And Sylvester the Stubborn Squirrel was lifting weights.

"What are you all doing here?" asked Ziggy.

"We decided to run in the Zig-Zag Race," said Delilah. "We'd like to win the ride in the zeppelin, too."

"But the race is next week!" said Ziggy. "It takes a long time to get in shape, and you haven't been exercising very much. Why not start preparing now for next year's race? That's the right way to do it."

"No way!" said Ivy. "A year is too long to wait. We're running in this year's race. One week is plenty of time to get ready."

"If we work hard all week," said Emmy, "we'll be just as ready as Ziggy!"

"Yes," everyone agreed.

So for the rest of the week, the AlphaPets tried to get in shape. But they did too much, too fast.

Emmy wanted to lose weight so she didn't eat much at all. After a few days, she was too weak to move.

Herbie and Monty did so many sit-ups that after a few days, they were too sore to move!

Sylvester jumped rope so much that after a few days, he was too tired to move!

And Ivy ate so many bowls of super-nutritious cereal that after a few days, she was too stuffed to move!

All week Ziggy kept exercising too, but not with his usual zip. He was worried. "What if I'm not good enough to win? What if someone beats me and I lose?" he thought.

Later that week while Ziggy was delivering the mail, he stopped at Wendy the Wise Woodchuck's house.

"What's the matter?" asked Wendy. "You don't seem your usual zippy self."

"I'm afraid I might not win the race," said Ziggy.

"You need to have confidence in yourself, Ziggy," Wendy said. "You're the most fit of all the AlphaPets. Just do the very best you can and you're bound to win!"

"Do you really think so?" Ziggy asked.

"Sure!" said Wendy. "Half of winning is believing you can win, and the rest is trying your hardest."

Then she added, "Even if you don't win, you'll know you did your best. And that's a kind of winning too."

That evening Ziggy felt much better. He wasn't worried and he didn't have the jitters. He continued preparing for the race as he always had done.

After a nutritious dinner, Ziggy took a bath and went to bed earlier than usual. "If I'm going to win tomorrow, I need plenty of sleep," he thought as he turned out the light.

When Ziggy finally fell asleep, he dreamed he was the pilot of a big zeppelin.

On the morning of the race, Ziggy was the first to arrive at the Zig-Zag Health Club. He was doing his warm-up exercises when Tina and Ollie arrived.

"Hey, Ziggy," shouted Tina. "Are you ready for the big race? To tell you the truth, I'm sure I'm going to win. I've been exercising and eating right all month."

"So have I," said Ollie. "This year there's going to be a
new winner—me!"

This time Ziggy didn't get the jitters. He just smiled
politely and said, "May the best runner win."

Soon all the runners gathered at the starting line.

"Three . . . two . . . one . . . they're off," shouted Vinnie the Vocal Vulture. The AlphaPets zigged and zagged between gates. They zigged and zagged over wooden horses. And they zigged and zagged all around the winding course.

Halfway through the race, Ivy and Herbie were in the lead. Then Tina and Ollie huffed and puffed by them. Ziggy was in fifth place, but he felt good. He wasn't tired and he wasn't out of breath. "I'm doing the best I can," he said to himself. "I know I can win. I know I can win!"

    Ziggy kept on running. He ran past Herbie and then
Ivy. But Ollie and Tina were ahead of him.

    "They're nearing the finish line, folks!" Vinnie shouted.
"Ziggy is now running neck and neck with Tina and
Ollie. Who will have the zeal and the zest to win this
long hard race?"

As Ziggy came around the last turn, he could see the finish line. He also noticed that Tina and Ollie were slowing down.

"I can make it! *I'm* going to win this race," he said to himself. Then he took a deep breath and ran as fast as he could go.

He ran past Ollie, past Tina, and straight across the finish line.

"Hurray for Ziggy! He's the zippiest!" everyone shouted.

When the race was over, Vinnie handed Ziggy the gold trophy and said, "It gives me great pleasure . . . great pleasure indeed, to award this trophy to you, Ziggy. You've won not one, not two, but *three* years in a row. Yes, indeed! What's your winning secret, dear friend?"

"Secret? It's no secret," said Ziggy. "You must eat healthful foods and get plenty of exercise every day . . . not just the week or the month before a race. And you should always get plenty of sleep, too. But just as important," Ziggy said as he put his arm around Wendy, "is believing in yourself and doing the best you can!"

Ziggy winked at Wendy and added, "Everybody who does his best is a winner, so you must all join me for the ride in the zeppelin!"

The AlphaPets cheered and lifted Ziggy onto their shoulders.

"Hooray for Ziggy, he's the Zippiest!" they shouted.

"Zowie!" said Ziggy. "Now put me *down* so we can go *up* in the zeppelin!"

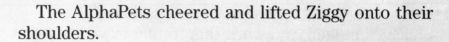

Zowie! Do your best to remember these zippy words with me.

zip code

zinnias

Emmy
the Exaggerating
Elephant

Fenton
the Fearful Frog

Gertie
the Grungy Goat

Herbie
the Happy
Hamster

Ivy
the Impatient
Iguana

Ollie
the Obedient
Ostrich

Perry
the Polite
Porcupine

Queenie
the Quiet Quail

Rupert
the Resourceful
Rhinoceros

Wendy
the Wise
Woodchuck

Xavier
the X-ploring
Xenops

Yori
the Yucky Yak

Ziggy
the Zippy Zebra

NOTE TO PARENTS

Delilah's Delightful Dream
A story about cooperation

In this story, Delilah the Demanding Duck wants her AlphaPet friends to help clean up a messy vacant lot, but her bossy demands get her nowhere. When Delilah learns to ask for help in a friendly way, everyone pitches in and together they turn a "disgraceful, disgusting, dump" into a delightfully beautiful park.

In addition to enjoying this inspiring story with your child, you can use it to teach a gentle lesson about the important value of cooperation: working together harmoniously to achieve a common goal.

You can also use this story to introduce the letter **D**. As you read about Delilah the Demanding Duck, ask your youngster to listen for all the **D** words and point to the objects that begin with **D**. When you've finished reading the story, your child will enjoy doing the activity at the end of the book.

DRIFTWOOD PUBLIC LIBRARY
801 SW HWY. 101
LINCOLN CITY, OREGON 97367

The AlphaPets™ characters were conceived and created by Ruth Lerner Perle.
Characters interpreted and designed by Deborah Colvin Borgo.
Cover design by the Antler & Baldwin Design Group.
Book design and production by Publishers' Graphics, Inc.
Logo design by Deborah Colvin Borgo and Nancy S. Norton.

Grolier Books is a Division of Grolier Enterprises, Inc.   Printed and Manufactured in the United States of America

Copyright © 1990 by Graymont Enterprises, Inc. No part of this work may be reproduced or adapted in any manner or medium whatever without the express written permission of Graymont Enterprises, Inc. AlphaPets and the AlphaPets characters are trade and service marks of Graymont Enterprises, Inc.